PRO SPORTS SUPERSTARS

SUPERSTARS OF THE PITTSBURGH STEELERS

by M.K. Osborne

AMICUS | AMICUS INK

Amicus High Interest and Amicus Ink are imprints of Amicus
P.O. Box 1329, Mankato, MN 56002
www.amicuspublishing.us

Copyright © 2019. International copyright reserved in all countries. No part of this book may be reproduced in any form without written permission from the publisher.

Library of Congress Cataloging-in-Publication Data
Names: Osborne, M. K., author.
Title: Superstars of the Pittsburgh Steelers / by M. K. Osborne.
Description: Mankato, MN : Amicus, 2019. | Series: Pro sports superstars NFL | Includes bibliographical references and index. | Audience: K to grade 3.
Identifiers: LCCN 2017057750 (print) | LCCN 2017059316 (ebook) | ISBN 9781681514925 (pdf) | ISBN 9781681514109 (library binding : alk. paper) | ISBN 9781681523309 (pbk. : alk. paper)
Subjects: LCSH: Pittsburgh Steelers (Football team)--Biography--Juvenile literature. | Pittsburgh Steelers (Football team)--History--Juvenile literature. | Football players--United States--Biography--Juvenile literature.
Classification: LCC GV956.P57 (ebook) | LCC GV956.P57 M674 2019 (print) | DDC 796.332/640974886--dc23 LC record available at https://lccn.loc.gov/20170577500

Photo Credits: All photos from Associated Press except Getty Images/Joe Robbins 4–5, 10-11, Focus on Sport 6–7, George Gojkovich 12–13; Cal Sport Media/Alamy 18–19

Series designer: Veronica Scott
Book designer: Peggie Carley
Photo researcher: Holly Young

Printed in China
HC 10 9 8 7 6 5 4 3 2 1
PB 10 9 8 7 6 5 4 3 2 1

TABLE OF CONTENTS

Get to Know the Steelers 4

Joe Greene. 7

Terry Bradshaw 8

Hines Ward 11

Troy Polamalu 12

Ben Roethlisberger. 15

Antonio Brown 17

Le'Veon Bell 18

Young Star 21

Team Fast Facts 22

Words to Know 23

Learn More 24

Index 24

GET TO KNOW THE STEELERS

The Pittsburgh Steelers joined the **NFL** in 1933. They have the most Super Bowl wins in the NFL. The Steelers have played in eight Super Bowls. They have won six.

Who were some of the Steelers' greatest stars? Let's find out!

JOE GREENE

Joe Greene was on **defense**. He was strong and fast. Most of all, he was a great leader and team player. He helped the Steelers win four Super Bowls. He played in 10 **Pro Bowls**.

TERRY BRADSHAW

Terry Bradshaw was a great **quarterback.** He was known for his strong arm. He led the Steelers to four Super Bowl wins. He was the NFL Super Bowl **MVP** two years in a row, in 1978 and 1979.

Ward retired as a player in 2012. He came back to coach the Steelers in 2017.

HINES WARD

Hines Ward played **offense**. He was fast. He was good at catching passes. He helped the Steelers win two Super Bowls. He was even named Super Bowl MVP in 2006. Ward played in four Pro Bowls.

TROY POLAMALU

Troy Polamalu was a great **tackler.** He played in eight Pro Bowls. He helped the Steelers win two Super Bowls. Polamalu played for the Steelers for 12 years. He retired in 2015.

Roethlisberger is the youngest quarterback to win a Super Bowl.

BEN ROETHLISBERGER

Ben Roethlisberger is a great quarterback. He joined the Steelers in 2004. He is a good leader. He led the Steelers to two Super Bowl wins. He has played in five Pro Bowls.

ANTONIO BROWN

Antonio Brown is a wide receiver. He was a **rookie** in 2010. He is quick. He is good at catching the ball. He has been to five Pro Bowls. The last was in 2016.

LE'VEON BELL

Le'Veon Bell is on offense. He is a good runner and pass catcher. He was the Steelers' MVP of the 2014 season. He has been to two Pro Bowls.

Bell set a Steelers team record for the most receptions by a running back in the 2014 season.

YOUNG STAR

T.J. Watt is a linebacker. He hits hard. He is a good blocker. The Steelers picked him in the first round of the 2017 draft. His two brothers are also NFL football players.

Let's watch and see who will be the next star of the Steelers!

TEAM FAST FACTS

Founded: 1933

Home Stadium: Heinz Field (Pittsburgh, Pennsylvania)

Super Bowl Titles: 6 (1975, 1976, 1979, 1980, 2006, and 2009)

Nicknames: Men of Steel and The Black and Gold

Hall of Fame Players: 22 including Joe Greene, Terry Bradshaw, and Jack Lambert

Other Names Pittsburgh Pirates (1933-1939)

WORDS TO KNOW

defense – the group of players that tries to stop the other team from scoring

MVP – Most Valuable Player; an honor given to the best player each season

NFL – National Football League; the league pro football players play in

offense – the group of players that tries to score

Pro Bowl – the NFL's all-star game

quarterback – a player whose main jobs are to lead the offense and throw passes

rookie – a player in his first season

tackler – a player whose main job is knocking players on the other team to the ground so they cannot score

LEARN MORE

Books

Burgess, Zach. *Meet the Pittsburgh Steelers.* Chicago: Norwood House Press, 2017.

Morey, Allan. *The Pittsburgh Steelers Story.* Minneapolis: Bellwether Media, Inc., 2017.

Websites

NFL.com
http://nfl.com
Check out pictures and your favorite football players' stats.

NFL Rush
http://www.nflrush.com
Play games and learn how to be a part of NFL PLAY 60.

Steelers Kids Zone
http://www.steelers.com/community/kids-zone.html
Learn more about the Pittsburgh Steelers.

Every effort has been made to ensure that these websites are appropriate for children. However, because of the nature of the Internet, it is impossible to guarantee that these sites will remain active indefinitely or that their contents will not be altered.

INDEX

Bell, Le'Veon, 19
Bradshaw, Terry, 8
Brown, Antonio, 17

Greene, Joe, 7

leader, 7, 15

MVP, 8, 11, 18

NFL, 4, 8, 21

Polamalu, Troy, 12
Pro Bowl, 7, 11, 12, 15, 17, 18

Roethlisberger, Ben, 14, 15

Super Bowl, 4, 7, 8, 11, 12, 14, 15

Ward, Hines, 10, 11
Watt, T.J., 21